W9-BKF-223

Hello, Hello, Are You There, God?

MOLLY CONE

Illustrated by

Rosalind Charney Kaye

UAHC PRESS · NEW YORK, NEW YORK

For Nathan, Hannah,
Sarah, and Samuel

Library of Congress Cataloging-in-Publication Data

Cone, Molly.
Hello, hello, are you there, God? / Molly Cone :
illustrated by Rosalind Charney Kaye.
p.   cm.
Summary: Uses stories and illustrations to explain Jewish
traditions and instill a sense of identity in Jewish children.
ISBN 0-8074-0648-1 (pbk. : alk. paper)
1. God (Judaism—Juvenile literature.   2. Jews—Identity—
Juvenile literature.   3. Learning—Juvenile literature.
[1. Jews.   2. Judaism.]   I. Kaye, Rosalind Charney, ill.
II. Title.
BM610C56   1999
296.3'11—dc21   98-54754
                                                  CIP
                                                  AC

This book is printed on acid-free paper.
Copyright © 1971, 1972, 1973, 1999 by Molly Cone
Manufactured in the United States of America
10 9 8 7 6 5 4 3 2 1

Contents

The Words of the *Shema* v
If You Are Jewish vii

Part One · About God

Why Can't I See God? 5
The Fish That Looked for Water

How Do I Talk to God? 7
The Boy and the Flute

How Does God Talk to Us? 9
The Baby Mouse

How Does God Help Us? 13
The Father

Does God Know Me? 15
The Man Who Was Not Himself

Part Two · About Belonging

My Name Is Israel   23
We Help One Another   25
We Help God   29
We Are the People Who Live by Torah   31
I Belong   35

Part Three · About Learning

A Leader Is for Teaching   41
Yesterday Is for Remembering   43
Torah Is for Learning   47
Wisdom Is for Knowing   49
A Heart Is for Caring   53
Learning Is for Living   55

The Words of the Shema

שְׁמַע יִשְׂרָאֵל יְיָ אֱלֹהֵינוּ יְיָ אֶחָד

Shema Yisrael Adonai Eloheinu Adonai Echad.
Hear, O Israel, *Adonai* is our God, *Adonai* is One.

If You Are Jewish

The words of the *Shema*
are very special words
if you are Jewish.

You say them
when you go to bed at night
and when you get up
in the morning.

You say them in the synagogue
at many prayer services,
at Sabbath services,
and on the holy days, too.

You say them
at your consecration,
at your confirmation,
and often when you become bar or bat mitzvah.

Jews sing the words
to celebrate peace;
they say them as a prayer
when they must go to war.

They were the words that Moses said
after he taught God's commandments to the Children of Israel.

They were the words that Rabbi Akiva said
when he was put to death
by the enemies of the Jews.

The words of the *Shema*
are inside every *mezuzah* you see.
Jewish people
have been saying them
since Judaism began.

PART ONE

About God

About God

There is no number for God listed in the telephone book. There is no address for God listed anywhere. You can't reach God by telephone, mail, fax, or E-mail. Yet people hear God and talk to God all the time.

God doesn't speak in the way your friends, your family, or your teachers speak to you. You can't hear God through your ears or see God with your eyes. God is not a man with a long beard or a woman in a white gown. God is not a person. No one knows what God looks like.

Though you can't see God, you can see and hear God all around you. You see God when you see flowers growing, babies smiling, birds flying, fish swimming, and leaves dying. You see God in friendship and giving and caring. God is as real as love—as real as courage and kindness and hope.

When you say the Shema,
you are saying Hello to God.

The Fish That Looked for Water

One day a fish was swimming close to shore. "Water is the most important thing in the world," he heard someone say. "Without water there can be no life."

"I wonder where water is!" thought the little fish. He began to swim around looking for it.

He looked close to the bottom of the river.

He looked close to the top. He looked behind the plants and under the rocks.

"Where is water?" he called out to a fish swimming by. But that fish could not tell him.

He asked another fish, "Say, where can I find water?" But she did not know, either.

Farther and farther the little fish went out into the ocean. He asked fish after fish, "Where is water?" But not one of them knew.

The little fish went deeper and deeper into the ocean. There he met a wise old fish. "Did you ever hear of water?" he asked.

"Sure," said the wise old fish. "You can't live without it."

"That's right!" said the little fish. "But where is it?"

The old fish blinked. "It's all about you," he said. "It's all under you and over you and in you and around you."

The little fish laughed and swam away. And perhaps he is still swimming around and asking— "Where is water? Where is water?"

. . . .

The Boy and the Flute

Once there was a shepherd boy who made a willow flute.

He played to his sheep. He played to his goats. And sometimes just for the fun of it, he played to himself.

One day, very early in the morning, he led his sheep to a pond. He heard frogs singing.

"Listen!" he said to his flock. Then he put the willow flute to his lips and played the sound of the frogs.

One day, even earlier in the morning, the boy led his sheep to the top of a hill. He saw the sun rise.

"Listen!" he said to his flock. Then he put the willow flute to his lips and played the sound of the sun rising.

One day he went home a different way. He passed a synagogue. Chanting came from inside. The shepherd boy stopped to listen.

"What are they doing?" he asked a person passing by.

"They are praying," the person said.

The shepherd boy listened for a long time. Then he opened the door and went in. He had never been inside a synagogue before.

Everyone was swaying back and forth. All were reading out loud from the prayer books in their hands.

The shepherd boy picked up a prayer book. He, too, began to sway to the sound of the prayers.

Suddenly he also wanted to pray. But he did not know the words. So he put down the book and raised the flute to his lips. He blew. He played the sound he was feeling in his heart.

Everyone stopped praying. Some turned and frowned. Frightened, the shepherd boy put down his flute. "I don't know how to read words," he said. "I just know how to play notes."

The rabbi looked at him over all the heads of the congregation. He smiled at the boy. "You have made a true prayer," the rabbi said, "for it came from your heart."

The shepherd boy looked at his flute in surprise. Then he smiled, too.

HOW DOES GOD TALK TO US?

. . . .

The Baby Mouse

A baby mouse came into this world and cried,
"Mama, Mama, where are you?"

"Open your eyes," said a soft voice. The baby mouse opened his eyes and saw his mother. "Your eyes are to see with," his mother said.

And the little mouse went back to sleep. A little later something else woke him. He opened his eyes wide. "Mama, Mama," he cried. "I can't see it!"

"Hush," she said soothingly. "You can see with your ears, too. Listen!"

So the little mouse listened and heard a curious whoosh.

"That is the wind," said his mother. "Now go back to sleep."

A while later the little mouse awoke again. "Mama," he cried. "What is that? I can't see it with my eyes, and I can't see it with my ears."

"My child, you can see with your nose, too. See!" she sniffed. "That is the smell of smoke coming from a house chimney."

"Oh," said the mouse, and he went back to sleep.

Soon he woke up again. He looked with his eyes, and he listened with his ears, and he sniffed with his nose. But he could not see what gave him that curious feeling. "Mama, Mama," he cried. And he cried and cried.

"Good gracious, child, you must be hungry," said his mother. "Your stomach has eyes, too," she told him. And she gave him some milk. The little field mouse ate and went back to sleep.

Suddenly a sharp pinch woke him. "You can see with your feelings, too," his mother taught him. "And each time you learn something new, you are seeing with your mind," she said.

"I have learned to see a great deal," said the little mouse proudly. "I guess I am all grown up."

But his mother shook her head. "Not yet," she said. "You still have something important to see."

One day the little mouse left the nest. Suddenly he came upon a baby bird that hadn't yet learned to fly. The baby bird saw the little mouse and began to run back and forth.

The little mouse felt a very strange feeling.

"Don't be afraid," he said to the bird. "I won't hurt you." And he ran home.

"Mama, Mama," he cried. "I saw a little bird that couldn't fly and it was afraid of me. So I quickly ran away."

His mother smiled. "Now you have seen with your heart," she said.

And the little mouse knew he had learned to see the most important way of all.

. . . . . .

The Father

Once there was a king who loved his young son more than anything in the world. But the queen had died and the king had to leave his child for a time.

"Have you taken good care of my son?" he asked his servants when he returned.

"Oh yes, yes!" they said proudly. "I feed him myself every day," said the cook. "I wash and dress him," said the little maid. "I button and buckle and tie," said the hired boy. "I pull him in his little blue wagon wherever he wants to go," said the gardener.

"We do everything for him!" they said all together.

But the king frowned. "Bring that child to me!" he shouted.

The cook and the nurse and the maid and the hired boy and the gardener all ran to the nursery. "Quick! Quick!" they said. "Your father, the king, wants to see you!"

The baby prince yawned. He let them dress him and button him and comb him and set him in his little wagon and take him to the king, his father.

The king saw that his son was quite old enough to walk. He set the child on his own two feet.

The servants gasped. "Oh, we have not let him walk yet, Sir!" said the maid. "He might hurt himself!" said the cook.

The king held out his arms to the child. "Come to me," he said.

The young prince looked at his father, then back at the blue wagon.

"I will help you," said the father.

The child stood there, tottering. The servants held their breath. The cook threw her apron over her head so that she would not see him fall.

"Come," said the father. And the young prince lifted a foot and took a step.

Quietly the father moved a step back. "Come," he said again. The child looked toward the safety of his father's arms. He took another step.

The father stepped back again. Then with a little laugh, the prince took two more steps and fell into his father's arms.

"Good!" the king said and held his child tightly. "Now you have begun to learn to walk!"

The servants looked at the king in awe.

"I helped him to help himself," the king said. "That is what helping is for."

· · · · · · ·

The Man Who Was Not Himself

Eli sat at the door of his house. Inside his wife sang to herself. But Eli only sat and sighed. He was watching his neighbor, Mr. Jonathan.

Mr. Jonathan wore his hair parted in the middle and had a beard on his chin. He smiled with one side of his mouth and winked one eye when he talked. He talked in a loud, strong voice.

Mr. Jonathan had a gold tooth in the front of his mouth. He had a red rosebush in the front of his house.

People invited Mr. Jonathan to lunch and to dinner. They sent him big boxes of fruit or candy on the holidays. Eli wished that he were Mr. Jonathan instead of Eli.

Eli started to part his hair in the middle. He began to grow a beard.

His wife said with a laugh, "If you don't watch out, you'll be getting to look just like Mr. Jonathan."

Eli smiled, with one side of his mouth. He began to wink one eye when he talked. He began to say "Good morning!" in a loud, strong voice.

His wife began to look at him with a wrinkle in her forehead.

Eli came home one day with a rosebush—a red one, just like Mr. Jonathan's. The next day he came home with a gold tooth in the front of his mouth.

Whenever Mr. Jonathan said the day was too hot, Eli said the day was too hot. When Mr. Jonathan said business was bad, Eli said business was

bad. When Mr. Jonathan admitted to a liking for broccoli, suddenly broccoli became Eli's favorite food.

One day Mr. Jonathan was sick in bed. The very next day Eli said that he was sick, too.

His wife began to cry and ran to get the rabbi. "He's still in bed," Mrs. Eli told the rabbi at noontime. "He says he's sick just like Mr. Jonathan."

The rabbi came and sat down next to Eli's bed. "Poor Mr. Jonathan," he said.

"Why do you say 'poor' Mr. Jonathan?" Eli complained. "Why don't you say 'poor' Eli?"

The rabbi gazed at Eli's face. Then he looked out the window at the red rosebush in Eli's front yard. "Poor Eli," the rabbi said with a sigh.

Eli looked at him suspiciously. "Look into the mirror," said the rabbi.

Eli sat up and looked into the mirror. On his face he saw Mr. Jonathan's smile. On his chin he saw Mr. Jonathan's beard. In his mouth he saw Mr. Jonathan's gold tooth. And behind the smile, the beard, and the gold tooth, he saw himself looking back.

"God made every person different from every other person," said the rabbi. "In all the world, there is only one Mr. Jonathan."

Eli stared at the foolish face in the mirror. He grimaced.

". . . and there is only one Eli," said the rabbi.

"Thanks to God," said Eli's wife, raising her eyes to the heavens.

And with a shamefaced smile, Eli rolled out of bed.

About Belonging

About Belonging

Being Jewish has nothing to do with the color of your skin, the shape of your nose, the way your hair curls, or the country in which you were born. It is not a nationality, it is not a race, and it is more than a religion.

Every Jew, say the rabbis, is four thousand years old. If you are Jewish, you are Abraham challenging the idea of gods made of clay. If you are Jewish, you are Miriam singing and dancing after crossing the Sea of Reeds. If you are Jewish, you are Jacob wrestling with the questions and fears and ambitions inside you.

Being Jewish is many things that have to do with teachings handed down to you from all those who were Jews before you. It is many things that have to do with the way you behave, the way you think, and the way you live.

Being Jewish is being a member of a very large family called the Children of Israel, which began with the belief in One God.

When you say the Shema, *you are saying*
you belong to the family of the Jewish people.

My Name Is Israel

Jacob and Esau were brothers. They were twins, but they were not at all alike.

Esau was strong like a bear. Everyone admired him. His hair was red and thick. His shoulders were broad. His face was handsome. He was a good hunter and a good fighter.

Jacob was not as big as his brother. He did not like killing anything or fighting anyone. He liked to figure things out and to think. He liked to dream about making things better.

Esau was their father's favorite. Jacob envied Esau. He wished he were as strong.

Their mother said to Jacob, "You are just as strong as Esau. But you have a different kind of strength. Yours is on the inside."

Esau heard this and laughed very loud. Jacob was not a fighter like him. Esau could not see what kind of strength Jacob had.

"God sees it," said their mother. "When Jacob grows up, you will see it, too."

Esau paid no attention. He was proud of his outside strength. He spent most of his time wrestling with his friends to make himself grow even stronger.

Jacob wrestled, too, but not in the same way. Jacob wrestled inside, with himself. When he was afraid of Esau, he fought his fear. When he was jealous of their father's love for Esau, he fought his jealousy. When he was in a hurry to be done with his work, he fought his impatience. This made his kind of strength grow, too.

Sometimes Jacob did what was right, but sometimes he tried to fool people. At those times he wrestled with his angry feelings and his secret wishes.

The struggle went on inside him all the time he was a boy. And he kept growing stronger.

One day Jacob awoke feeling sure of himself and unafraid. The wrestling inside him had stopped. He was a full-grown man. Everybody began to see the kind of strength Jacob had. Jacob used his heart and his mind instead of his fists. He fought unfairness and ignorance and unkindness.

"I am strong," Esau said, "but Jacob is stronger. I can knock a man down and make him afraid, but Jacob can give a man courage."

People honored Jacob. They said he had wrestled with an angel of God and won a new name.

But Jacob knew he had wrestled not only with an angel. All the time he was growing up, he had wrestled with God inside himself. And if he had won a new name, there was only one name it could be.

"My name is Israel," Jacob said. Israel is a Hebrew word. It means "to struggle with God."

Jacob became the father of twelve sons and one daughter. "We are the Children of Israel," said they.

All their sons and daughters called themselves the Children of Israel, too. So did all the sons and daughters who followed.

Forever after, Israel was their name.

We Help One Another

A man came riding on his donkey into the land where the Children of Israel lived. He did not know these people. He had never bothered to come this way before. As he rode, he looked around curiously.

He passed a harvested field of wheat and then another. He saw that the workers were reaping nothing from the corners of the field.

"Who is the owner of these fields?" he asked one of them.

"*Adonai* owns them all," the worker said.

"Is this owner so rich that he does not reap the corners of his field?"

"*Adonai* commands that the corners be left for the traveler and the poor," the worker said.

"In that case," said the man, "I will help myself." And although he was neither a traveler nor poor, he piled his donkey high with wheat from the corners. Then he urged his little beast onward.

Soon he came to a grape orchard. The rider saw that many grapes had been left on the vines.

"Does the owner of the wheat field own the orchard, too?" he called to a woman carrying grapes in a basket.

"*Adonai* owns every field you see," said the woman. "But the grapes left on the vines belong to anyone in need."

The man made a sad face."There is no one more needy than I," he said. Then he greedily filled a basket full and added it to the donkey's load. He

intended to get away with his loot as quickly as possible. But he said craftily, "Where is the owner of these fields? I want to thank him."

"*Adonai,* the God of Israel, is everywhere," said the woman. "God owns all the earth and everything in it."

The man stared at her.

"We give our thanks," she said, "by sharing what we harvest. We call it *ma'asim tovim.*"

The man tried to hide the grin that curled up his mouth. He kicked his heels into the overloaded donkey's side to make the beast move along.

The woman called after him, "We give our thanks, too, by remembering to be kind to our animals."

But he pretended that he hadn't heard.

At the border of the village, he stopped to look back. Then he scratched his head and gave out a bellow of a laugh.

"What a crazy bunch of people they are," he said and continued on his way.

We Help God

Once there was a man named Micah. He saw the Children of Israel growing careless and greedy. He saw them being wasteful and forgetful.

"These are not the ways of God," he told them.

Many only laughed at him.

"Remember your God," Micah warned. "Or you may destroy yourselves."

Some laughed again but not quite so loud. And some began to be afraid.

"I will make a sacrifice to God!" one said. And quickly he took his neighbor's lamb as a gift to please God.

"I will make a sacrifice, too," said another. And in his hurry, he took a bleating calf from its mother as a gift to please God.

"I will make a bigger sacrifice!" said another loudly. And he took the ram that was the father of all his sheep as a gift to please God.

"I will make the biggest sacrifice of all!" someone else shouted. And he took oil from his warehouse to light and make a great show to please God.

Micah only shook his head more and more sadly.

A woman cried out, "But I have no calves, no rams, no oil. What can I do to please God?" And the tears began to run down her cheeks.

"Think," Micah said to her. "What would God want with calves? What would God want with gifts of thousands of rams? What would God want even with tens of thousands of rivers of oil?"

The woman stopped crying and started to think. That was true, she thought. God needed none of that. All of it had come from God.

"Then what does God want of us?" she asked.

Micah said, "Only to do good and to love mercy and to walk humbly."

"Oh," said the woman. And she looked at the one who had not done good by stealing his neighbor's lamb.

"Oh, oh," said the woman. And she looked at the two who had not loved mercy by taking a young calf from its mother and an old ram from its flock.

"Oh, oh, oh," said the woman. And she looked at the man who did not walk humbly but thought to make himself more important with a great show.

Micah went up and down the land saying the same words again and again. The Children of Israel listened. They called Micah a prophet because he spoke for God.

We Are the People
Who Live by Torah

Long ago there was an emperor who ordered everyone to worship him. But the Jews would not. So the emperor made a law against teaching Torah.

Rabbi Akiva paid no attention to the emperor's law. He went right on teaching. But every day fewer and fewer of his students came to learn.

One day Rabbi Akiva opened his door and only one student stood before him.

"The others were afraid to come," the boy said.

"Aren't you afraid, too?" asked Rabbi Akiva.

The boy nodded. "Everyone says we are not safe if we study Torah."

The rabbi sighed.

"I have come," the boy said, "but I must not listen." And he came in with his hands over his ears.

"Take your hands off your ears and I will tell you a story," Rabbi Akiva said.

The student took his hands off his ears and put them into his pockets. And the rabbi told the student this story:

Once there was a fox who was very hungry. He stood on the bank of a river. And the river was full of fish.

"Why do you move so fast and jump about?" the fox called to the fish.

"We are afraid of the fishermen's nets," the little fish called back.

"Why don't you jump up here with me?" said the fox. "There are no nets here on dry land!" And the fox licked his lips greedily.

The little fish jumped high to look. "That is right!" they told one another. "There are no nets on land."

"Wait!" an older fish said. "Maybe we are not safe in the water, but we will surely die if we jump out!"

"So it is with the Jewish people," Rabbi Akiva said. "Without our Torah, Jews are like fish on dry land. We must go on with the study of Torah even if it is not always safe to do so."

The student took his hands out of his pockets. But he did not put them on his ears. He put them on his book.

"I am listening," he said.

I Belong

Once there was a young woman named Esther. She lived in the ancient land of Persia with her cousin, Mordecai. When King Ahasuerus saw Esther, he chose her to be his queen.

Mordecai was proud that his cousin was the queen of Persia. He went to the palace gates often to see her.

Now part of the king's court was a man named Haman. Haman was the chief minister. The king often turned to him for his opinion. And the king seldom questioned his advice. Haman was so filled with his own importance that he demanded that everyone who came to the palace gates bow to him.

But Mordecai would not. "I am a Jew," Mordecai said. "I will bow only to God."

Haman was so angry that he devised a plan of revenge. He told the king that the Jew Mordecai and his followers were plotting to take over the throne. On Haman's advice,the king issued a royal decree for the destruction of all the Jews in his kingdom.

Haman was happy. He himself chose the date for the death of the Jews. He chose it by drawing lots. Then he ordered gallows to be set up in front of the palace gates. The first Jew to die on the set day, he announced, would be the Jew called Mordecai.

Mordecai wept for his people. "I will go to the king," said Esther, "and plead for all the Jews in the kingdom."

"You cannot," warned Mordecai. "Not even you the queen can see the king without his bidding. Whoever approaches the king without being summoned faces death."

"If I perish, I perish!" said Queen Esther.

Esther went to see the king. And she did not die. Because of Esther, the king righted the wrong that Haman had tried to do. The Jewish people were saved from Haman's vengeful plan. And Haman died on the gallows he had ordered for Mordecai.

The Jews of Persia celebrated the day set for their death as a day of victory. They made the day of celebration a holiday. They called the holiday Purim. Purim is a Hebrew word that means a drawing of lots.

From that time on, Jews celebrated Purim wherever they lived. Every year on Purim, the story of Esther is told. And every time the story is told, a great rattling of noisemakers blots out the mention of Haman's name.

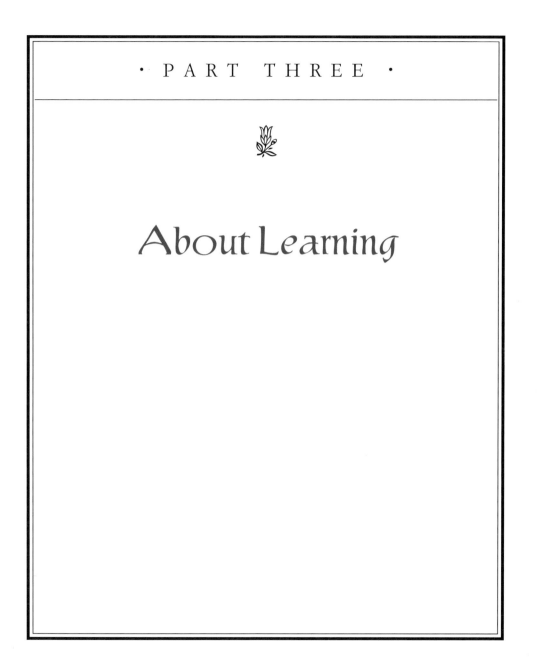

· PART THREE ·

About Learning

About Learning

God speaks to people through the words of the Torah. The Torah is the heart of Judaism.

For hundreds of years, Jewish people have bent their heads over the words of the Torah to grasp the meanings. The Torah is read and reread, week after week, month after month, and year after year. In every synagogue and temple around the world, the Scroll of the Torah is the Book of all books.

The Book tells not just one story—it tells everyone's story. It is a book of astonishments, a book of amazements, a book so wondrous that it fills the hearts and minds of its readers with awe. Most awesome of all is that every time the Torah is read, new meanings burst forth.

In the Jewish religion, learning is a holy activity. When you learn more about people and more about the earth, you are learning about God.

When you say the Shema, *all the*
wisdom in the Torah opens to you.

A Leader Is for Teaching

Moses was the leader of his people. They followed him out of a land of trouble. They followed him across a wide, wide desert. They followed him to the foot of a high and holy mountain. But they were afraid.

"How shall we live?" they cried. "What shall we do?"

"God will help us," Moses said. And Moses went up the mountain.

The people waited hopefully. "Perhaps Moses will return with sweet grapes and pomegranates," said one.

"Perhaps he will bring us a whole flock of lambs," said another.

"Perhaps he will bring a bag full of gold!" "Or maybe a box of jewels!"

The people began to laugh and clap and sing. "God will help us!" they shouted. "God will help us!"

Many days went by. "What will Moses bring us?" they kept saying. "What will he bring us?" They grew tired of waiting. And no one guessed what Moses did bring.

He came down the mountain. He came carrying two tablets of stone. "Hear these words!" he shouted. "They are the words of God!"

And Moses read what was written on the tablets of stone.

I am your God.
You shall have no other gods beside Me.
Remember the Sabbath day and keep it holy.

Honor your father and mother.
Do not murder.
Do not be unfaithful to your wife or husband.
Do not steal.
Do not tell false tales about another.
Do not want what belongs to your neighbor.

These were rules of fairness and kindness.
They were rules for living together in peace.
Moses taught them to the Children of Israel. They called him *Moshe Rabenu*—Moses, Our Teacher. They learned God's words by heart.
Forever after, they lived according to these laws they called Torah.

Yesterday Is for Remembering

Once there was a very young king who did not know very much about being a ruler. He did not know about God. He did not know about belonging. He did not know about learning. But he wanted to be a good king. He wanted to rule as well as David and Solomon, who had been kings long before him.

"How can I learn to be a good king?" he asked his counselors.

They smiled secretly at one another. "You can learn by doing just what we tell you," they said.

So young King Josiah did just what his counselors told him. And he saw that his counselors grew richer while his people grew poorer. And he knew that he had not learned how to be a good king.

He asked the court magicians, "How can I learn to be a good king?"

They smiled up at the stars. "Pray to the sun and the moon in the heavens," they said.

So King Josiah did what his magicians advised. And he saw that his people filled the Temple with idols. And he knew that he had not learned how to be a good king.

He asked the priests of the Temple, "How can I learn to be a good king?"

"The Temple is falling down!" they said. "The roof will soon be on our heads!"

So King Josiah called the workmen. They fixed the roof, mended the cracks in the walls, and made the Temple look like new again. But the king knew that he had not learned how to be a good king.

One day a workman brought a book to King Josiah. "I found it buried in the Temple wall," he said.

King Josiah looked at it curiously. It was very old. He began to read.

I am Adonai *your God who brought you out of the land of Egypt. . . . You shall have no other gods beside Me. . . .*

King Josiah read on and on. He read all the rules about fairness and kindness. And as he read, the tears began to run down his face.

They were the words Moses had taught his people. They were the same rules King David had followed. And King Solomon, too.

"Now they are my laws!" young King Josiah decreed. And he knew that he had finally learned to be a good king.

Torah Is for Learning

Long ago there lived a man named Ezra. He wrote down the Laws of Moses on a scroll of parchment. He wrote down all the rules that Moses had taught. When he finished, he rolled up the long scroll. He called it the *Sefer Torah*, the Scroll of the Torah.

One day Ezra went to the gates of the city. He took the *Sefer Torah* with him. He spoke out to all the people, "Hear, O Israel, *Adonai* is our God, *Adonai* is One."

Some stopped to listen.

"Hear the words of *Adonai*, our God!" Ezra called. "Teach them to your children. Say them when you sit in your house. And when you walk on your way. And when you go to sleep. And when you wake up...."

More people began to gather round. Ezra unrolled the *Sefer Torah*. He began to read what it said out loud. He read about God and the stone tablets, Moses and the Children of Israel, and all the rules that God had given them to live by.

And the people who had forgotten began to remember. "Amen, Amen," they said.

Every Sabbath and twice during the week, Ezra went to the gates of the city. He carried the *Sefer Torah* and read aloud from it. Every week more and more people came to listen and learn.

From that time on, the *Sefer Torah* has been read aloud week after week all through the year. Today people listen to the *Sefer Torah* in their synagogues and temples. It is read aloud every Sabbath, on holidays, and at other times, too.

Wisdom Is for Knowing

King Solomon was said to be the wisest ruler in all the world. It was said he understood the birds in the air and the beasts of the field. He knew all the languages of the earth. He could solve any problem. And he could answer any riddle.

One day the Queen of Sheba came to see this wise king. "Answer me a question," she said. "What made you so wise?"

King Solomon knew that this queen had both knowledge and wit. "My answer must please her," he said to himself. And this is how he answered the queen's question.

Once when I was very young, I dreamed a dream. I dreamed I heard God say, "Solomon! Make a wish, and it will come true!"

I did not know what to wish for. I thought of gold. I thought of silver. I thought of a castle full of jewels, or a kingdom twice bigger than my own.

Then what I should wish for came to me.

I would wish for something greater than gold or silver or castles or a bigger kingdom.

"I wish for an understanding heart," I said to God.

The queen leaned forward eagerly. "Then what happened?" she asked.

King Solomon smiled at the beautiful queen. "Why, then I woke up," he said.

The queen laughed. King Solomon was very wise, indeed. He had pleased her very much.

A Heart Is for Caring

One day two women came before wise King Solomon. Behind them followed a servant with a baby. Angrily one woman said, "This baby is mine! And this woman wants to take him from me!"

"Oh no!" said the other woman. "The baby is mine!"

King Solomon looked from one woman to the other. "But which of you is the mother?" "I am!" both answered at once.

The servant stepped up to explain. "Both their babies were born at the same time. Then one baby died." "Which one?" asked the king.

"Hers!" Each woman pointed to the other.

One was telling the truth, thought the king. And one was not. But which was which? All his knowledge could not help him. "Poor women!" he thought. He pitied them both. What was he to do?

King Solomon looked first at one woman and then at the other. Then he looked into his heart. Suddenly he knew the wise thing to do. He must find out which woman really loved this child.

"Bring me my sword!" he called very loudly. "I shall divide the baby in two," he said. "Then I shall give half to each of you."

One woman threw herself down at the king's feet. "Give my baby to her if you must! But do not hurt him!" she cried.

King Solomon put down his sword. He helped the woman up. He put the baby into her arms. "This child is yours," he said. "For now I know that you are his real mother."

Learning Is for Living

Once there was a learned man named Hillel. People came to Jerusalem from far-off places just to talk with him. And when they returned home, they went about repeating what the famous man had said.

"Hillel says, 'Do not judge your neighbor until you are in his place.'" And "Hillel says, 'The more schools, the more wisdom.'"

Hillel was a scholar of Torah. The Torah fills five books. And everyone said Hillel knew everything in them. Everyone said Hillel not only studied Torah, he followed its teachings every day. They said he could teach even those who didn't want to learn.

But once a stranger arrived in Jerusalem who did not believe what everyone said about Hillel. He believed no one was quite so clever as he himself was.

One day he stopped Hillel on the street. "So you are the scholar Hillel!" The stranger spoke loudly so that all the people around them would hear.

Hillel nodded.

"Teach me the Torah while I stand on one foot!" the man said. And he got ready for a good laugh.

Hillel did not even hesitate: "What is hateful to you, do not do to another," he said. "All the rest of Torah only explains this. Now go and learn."

And the great scholar left the stranger standing there with his foot still up in the air.